Tweezle into Everything

Stephanie McLellan
& Dean Griffiths

pajamapress

First published in the United States in 2014
Text copyright © Stephanie McLellan
Illustration copyright © Dean Griffiths
This edition copyright © 2013 Pajama Press

10 9 8 7 6 5 4 3 2 1

**Canada Council Conseil des arts
for the Arts du Canada**

**ONTARIO ARTS COUNCIL
CONSEIL DES ARTS DE L'ONTARIO**

The publisher gratefully acknowledges the support of the Canada Council for the Arts and the Ontario
Arts Council for its publishing program. We acknowledge the financial support of the Government of
Canada through the Canada Book Fund (CBF) for our publishing activities.

Library and Archives Canada Cataloguing in Publication

McLellan, Stephanie Simpson, 1959-, author
      Tweezle into everything / Stephanie McLellan ; illustrated
by Dean Griffiths.
ISBN 978-1-927485-47-7 (bound)
      I. Griffiths, Dean, 1967-, illustrator II. Title.
PS8575.L457T83 2013   jC813'.6   C2013-902732-7

Publisher Cataloging-in-Publication Data (U.S.)

McLellan, Stephanie, 1959-
      Tweezle into everything / Stephanie McLellan and Dean Griffiths.
[32] p. : col. ill. ;   cm.
Summary: Tweezle is a toddler who wants to be a big boy. But his family doesn't recognize how much
he has grown until Tweezle surprises them with a big idea to help a baby bird.
ISBN-978-1-927485-47-7
1. Siblings – Juvenile fiction. 2. Self -acceptance – Juvenile fiction. I. Griffiths, Dean, 1967- . II. Title.
[E] dc23   PZ7.M354Tw 2013

Manufactured by Sheck Wah Tong Printing Ltd.
Printed in Hong Kong, China.

Pajama Press Inc.
112 Berkeley St. Toronto, Ontario Canada, M5A 2W7
www.pajamapress.ca

Distributed in the U.S. by Orca Book Publishers
PO Box 468 Custer, WA, 98240-0468, USA

For the real Tweezle (aka Shmoe, aka Tristan), who
really did grow up to be big (as in tall!). And for
the rest of the JETS with my never-ending love.

    –S.M.

For my mum and dad

    –D.G.

Pumpkin was the first.
Hoogie came next.

Tweezle is the baby.

"My sweet baby boy," says Mom. "You're the pot of gold at the end of the rainbow."

"Up you go, baby boy!" says Dad.
"You're the last yummy cookie
in the cookie jar."

"I not baby," says Tweezle.
"I big boy!"

At breakfast, Pumpkin makes pancakes.

Hoogie makes a pretty bouquet
of flowers.

Tweezle makes a mess!

Mom is talking on the phone when she hears a **splash** and a **crash**.

"Tweezle?" she calls.

"Oh, Tweezle!" says Mom.
"Why would you do that?"

"I big!" says Tweezle, grinning.

Dad is taking a snooze when he hears
a **blam** and a **slam**.

"Yikes, Tweezle!" says Dad.
"What are you thinking?"

"I big," says Tweezle.

"Mom!" says Pumpkin. "Look what Tweezle did! That little rat drew all over my picture!"

"Dad!" yells Hoogie. "The little slug has been in my room! He wrecked my stuff!"

"I not little," sniffs Tweezle. "I big."

"You're the lint at the bottom of my pocket!" says Pumpkin.

"And the mud on the bottom of my sneakers!" says Hoogie.

"I not bottom," says Tweezle. "I big boy."

After dinner, Tweezle is missing.

Mom looks upstairs.

Dad looks downstairs.

Pumpkin and Hoogie look
in the backyard.

"Dad!" says Pumpkin. "Look what Tweezle did!"

"He dug a hundred holes!" says Hoogie.

"He's just into everything these days," says Mom.

"Where is that little monster?" says Dad.

Mom and Dad and Pumpkin and Hoogie
follow the muddy footprints.

"Hey!" says Pumpkin. "That's my basket!"

"Tweezle!" says Hoogie. "That's my blanket!"

"Wait a minute," says Mom.
"**Look** what Tweezle did!"

A baby bird nestles in Hoogie's blanket,
in Pumpkin's basket, in Tweezle's arms.

Tweezle hums a lullabye as he rocks
the baby bird back and forth.

"Baby fall," he says, pointing
at the empty nest in the tree.

"What a big thing to do!" says Mom.

"This is a big deal, Tweezle!" says Pumpkin.

"Where did you get such a big idea?" says Hoogie.

"Come here, big guy," says Dad. "Let's hang the basket where the mommy bird will find it."

Tweezle is bigger than everyone when
Dad lifts him onto his shoulders.

"You should be so proud of yourself!" says Mom.

"Big time," says Tweezle.